# 沙與沫

## SAND AND FOAM

哈里利·紀伯倫
Kahlil Gibran ——著

張家綺 ——譯

我永遠在海岸上行走，
就在那沙與沫之間，
高漲潮水將抹去我的足跡，
海風也將吹散泡沫，
唯獨海與岸留存佇立，
直到永遠。

1 #

I AM FOREVER walking upon these shores,

Betwixt the sand and the foam,

The high tide will erase my foot-prints,

And the wind will blow away the foam.

But the sea and the shore will remain

Forever.

2 #

我曾用手捕捉迷霧，

攤開手掌，霧氣是一條蟲。

合掌後再攤開，看哪，是隻鳥。

我的手合了又開，

空洞掌心中，有個男人神態哀戚地駐足仰望。

我合起手掌，再次打開，

手掌卻空無一物，只見一片薄霧，

然我卻聽見一首甜美動人的曲子。

2 #

Once I filled my hand with mist.

Then I opened it and lo, the mist was a worm.

And I closed and opened my hand again, and behold there was a bird.

And again I closed and opened my hand, and in its hollow stood a man with
a sad face, turned upward.

And again I closed my hand, and when I opened it there was naught but mist.

But I heard a song of exceeding sweetness.

4 #

他們清醒著對我說，

「你和你居住的世界，

不過是無垠海洋的無垠岸上，那一小粒沙。」

我在夢境裡告訴他們：

「我即是那片無垠海洋，

所有世界全是我岸上的顆顆細沙。」

3 #

昨日我以為我是一塊碎片，

在生命的穹蒼裡，不帶韻律地震顫。

今日我卻知曉，我即是那片穹蒼，

生命則如斑斑碎片，在我心底充滿節奏地流竄。

3 #

It was but yesterday I thought myself a fragment quivering without rhythm in the sphere of life.

Now I know that I am the sphere, and all life in rhythmic fragments moves within me.

4 #

They say to me in their awakening, "You and the world you live in are but a grain of sand upon the infinite shore of an infinite sea."

And in my dream I say to them, "I am the infinite sea, and all worlds are but grains of sand upon my shore."

5 ＃

今生我僅只一次無言以對，

那次，有個男人問我：

「你是誰？」

6 ＃

想到上帝，我們第一個念頭是天使。

形容上帝，我們第一個說法是人。

## 5 ＃

Only once have I been made mute. It was when a man asked me,
"Who are you?"

## 6 ＃

The first thought of God was an angel.
The first word of God was a man.

千千萬萬年前，
我們曾是振翅流浪、渴望依歸的生物，
直到大海與森林裡的風捎來話語。
而今我們該如何用昨日的聲音，
訴說我們古老的故事？

人面獅畢生只開過一次口：
「一粒沙即一片大漠，
一片大漠乃一粒沙；
現在讓我們再次緘默。」
人面獅的話語字字鏗鏘，我卻不解其意。

7 #

We were fluttering, wandering, longing creatures a thousand thousand years
before the sea and the wind in the forest gave us words.
Now how can we express the ancient of days in us with only the sounds of our
yesterdays?

8 #

The Sphinx spoke only once, and the Sphinx said, "A grain of sand is a
desert, and a desert is a grain of sand; and now let us all be silent again."
I heard the Sphinx, but I did not understand.

我仰臥在埃及的塵埃許久，

默不作聲，不曉四季更迭。

太陽誕下了我，我在尼羅河畔起身行走，

跟著白晝哼唱，隨著黑夜入夢。

如今太陽的千足爬過我軀體，

我可能將再化為埃及塵埃，

可是看啊，這是個奇蹟、也是個謎！

拼湊出我生命的太陽拆毀不了我。

於是我依然聳立，腳步堅定，

走在尼羅河畔。

9 #

Long did I lie in the dust of Egypt, silent and unaware of the seasons.

Then the sun gave me birth, and I rose and walked upon the banks of the Nile,

Singing with the days and dreaming with the nights.

And now the sun threads upon me with a thousand feet that I may lie again in the dust of Egypt.

But behold a marvel and a riddle!

The very sun that gathered me cannot scatter me.

Still erect am I, and sure of foot do I walk upon the banks of the Nile.

10 #

Remembrance is a form of meeting.

11 #

Forgetfulness is a form of freedom.

11 #

原諒即是一種自由。

10 #

懷念即是一種相見。

12 #

我們用數不盡的太陽行進掂酌歲月；
他們拿小小口袋裡的小機械斟算光陰。
告訴我，這樣的我們該如何在同一地點，同一時間相會？

12 #

We measure time according to the movement of countless suns; and they measure time by little machines in their little pockets.

Now tell me, how could we ever meet at the same place and the same time?

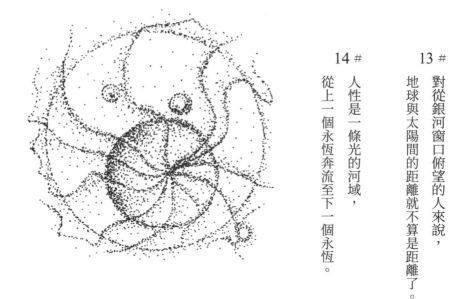

14 #

人性是一條光的河域，

從上一個永恆奔流至下一個永恆。

13 #

對從銀河窗口俯望的人來說，

地球與太陽間的距離就不算是距離了。

13 #

Space is not space between the earth and the sun to one
who looks down from the windows of the Milky Way.

14 #

Humanity is a river of light running from the ex-eternity to eternity.

## 15 #

永居於蒼穹裡的靈魂，

莫不羨妒人類的痛楚？

## 16 #

踏往聖城的途中，我遇見一名朝聖者，便問：

「此路確實是通往聖城之路？」

他道：「跟我來，你一日一夜後就會抵達聖城。」

我便隨著他的腳步，走過日日夜夜，卻始終不見聖城。

怎料他居然因為誤領我，對我忿懣不已。

## 15 #

Do not the spirits who dwell in the ether envy man his pain?

## 16 #

On my way to the Holy City I met another pilgrim and I asked him, "Is this indeed the way to the Holy City?"

And he said, "Follow me, and you will reach the Holy City in a day and a night."

And I followed him. And we walked many days and many nights, yet we did not reach the Holy City.

And what was to my surprise he became angry with me because he had misled me.

**17 #**

上帝啊，把兔子變成我的獵物前，
先讓我當獅子的獵物吧。

**18 #**

不走過黑夜幽徑，
哪得破曉晨光。

**19 #**

我的屋舍對我說：「別離我遠去，這裡住著你的過去。」
道路聲聲呼喚我：「快跟我來，我即是你的未來。」
我告訴屋舍與道路：「本人無過去，也無未來。
若我留下，留下終將離去；若我離去，離去也將留下。
唯獨愛與死能改變一切。」

## 17 #

Make me, oh God, the prey of the lion, ere You make the rabbit my prey.

## 18 #

One may not reach the dawn save by the path of the night.

## 19 #

My house says to me, "Do not leave me, for here dwells your past."

And the road says to me, "Come and follow me, for I am your future."

And I say to both my house and the road, "I have no past, nor have I a future. If I stay here, there is a going in my staying; and if I go there is a staying in my going. Only love and death will change all things."

沙與沫 Sand and Foam

20 #

若是枕著羽毛入眠的夢，
不比地面的夢美麗，
我又怎能對生命的公正失去信念？
怪哉，對某些快樂的想望，
竟成為我一部分的痛苦。

20 #

How can I lose faith in the justice of life, when the dreams of those who sleep
upon feathers are not more beautiful than the dreams of those who sleep upon the
earth? Strange, the desire for certain pleasures is a part of my pain.

我曾七度鄙視我的靈魂：

第一回，我看著她明可展翅高飛，卻不禁軟弱。

第二回，我看著她尚未瘸腿，就先跛行。

第三回，在難與易之間，她選擇了易。

第四回，她犯了錯，卻安慰自己人皆犯錯。

第五回，她因軟弱而壓抑，卻說耐性是種力量。

第六回，她鄙視臉容的醜陋，殊不知那也是她的一張面具。

第七回，她哼唱讚美歌，卻以為那就是美德。

## 21 #

Seven times have I despised my soul:

The first time when I saw her being meek that she might attain height.

The second time when I saw her limping before the crippled.

The third time when she was given to choose between the hard and the easy, and she chose the easy.

The fourth time when she committed a wrong, and comforted herself that others also commit wrong.

The fifth time when she forbore for weakness, and attributed her patience to strength.

The sixth time when she despised the ugliness of a face, and knew not that it was one of her own masks.

And the seventh time when she sang a song of praise, and deemed it a virtue.

24 #

天堂就近在隔壁門後的咫尺；
我卻丟失那把鑰匙，
抑或遺忘他方。

23 #

只有一樣東西能拉近想像力與成就之間的距離，
那就是一個人的渴望。

22 #

我對絕對的真相一無所知。
然面對無知，我卻謙遜，
這就是我的榮耀與報酬。

22 #

I AM IGNORANT of absolute truth. But I am humble before my ignorance and therein lies my honor and my reward.

23 #

There is a space between man's imagination and man's attainment that may only be traversed by his longing.

24 #

Paradise is there, behind that door, in the next room; but I have lost the key. Perhaps I have only mislaid it.

## 25 #

You are blind and I am deaf and dumb, so let us touch hands and understand.

## 26 #

The significance of man is not in what he attains, but rather in what he longs to attain.

26 #

一個人的重要性不在於他的功成名就，而是他對功成名就的渴求。

25 #

你目不可視，我耳不聰，口不語，且讓我們觸碰彼此的手，相互理解。

## 27 #

有人就像墨水，有人則如白紙。
若非他們的黑，我們豈會傻；
若非他們的白，我們豈能盲。

## 27 #

Some of us are like ink and some like paper.

And if it were not for the blackness of some of us,

some of us would be dumb;

And if it were not for the whiteness of some of us,

some of us would be blind.

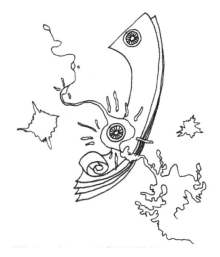

## 28 #

借我你的耳朵，
我就讓你聽我的聲音。

## 28 #

Give me an ear and I will give you a voice.

## 29 #

Our mind is a sponge; our heart is a stream.

Is it not strange that most of us choose sucking

rather than running?

## 30 #

When you long for blessings that you may not name,

and when you grieve knowing not the cause, then

indeed you are growing with all things that grow, and

rising toward your greater self.

## 29 #

我們的頭腦猶如海綿；我們的心靈宛若河川。

我們大都選擇吸收而不願奔流，豈不怪哉？

## 30 #

當你渴望無以名狀的祝福，當你哀痛不知所以的傷懷，

你就跟著生長的萬物成長，昇華成更高的自我。

31 #

當一個人沉醉於某個願景，
就把願景的朦朧畫面錯當美酒。

32 #

你啜飲讓你迷醉的酒；
我則喝下能讓我醒酒的飲料。

31 #

When one is drunk with a vision, he deems
his faint expression of it the very wine.

32 #

You drink wine that you may be intoxicated; and I
drink that it may sober me from that other wine.

33 #

當我的酒杯空蕩，我願服了它的空無；
但酒杯半滿時，我忿忿不平它的半滿。

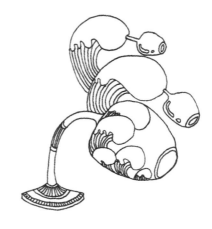

33 #

When my cup is empty I resign myself to its emptiness;
but when it is half full I resent its half-fulness.

## 34 #

一個人真實的面貌不是他讓你看見的一面，

而是他無法讓你看見的那一面。

若想認識真正的他，就切勿聽他說了什麼，

而是注意他沒說出口的。

## 34 #

The reality of the other person is not in what he
reveals to you, but in what he cannot reveal to you.
Therefore, if you would understand him, listen not to
what he says but rather to what he does not say.

## 35 #

我的話語有一半言不由衷；

但我還是要說，好讓另一半能抵達你心底。

## 35 #

Half of what I say is meaningless; but I say it
so that the other half may reach you.

## 36 #

幽默感是一種攸關比例調和的感受。

## 36 #

A sense of humour is a sense of proportion.

37 #

人們讚揚我聒噪的錯誤，
卻譴責我沉默的美德，
此時寂寞油然而生。

38 #

當人生找不到能夠高歌己心的伶人，
就誕生出一名傳達己意的哲學家。

## 37 #

My loneliness was born when men praised my talkative faults and blamed
my silent virtues.

## 38 #

When Life does not find a singer to sing her heart she produces a
philosopher to speak her mind.

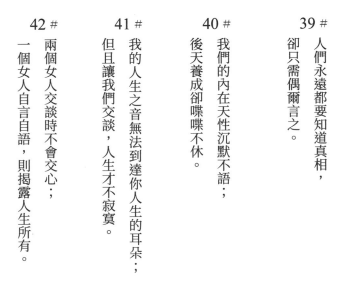

42 #

兩個女人交談時不會交心；

一個女人自言自語，則揭露人生所有。

41 #

我的人生之音無法到達你人生的耳朵；

但且讓我們交談，人生才不寂寞。

40 #

我們的內在天性沉默不語；

後天養成卻喋喋不休。

39 #

人們永遠都要知道真相，

卻只需偶爾言之。

## 39 #

A truth is to be known always, to be uttered sometimes.

## 40 #

The real in us is silent; the acquired is talkative.

## 41 #

The voice of life in me cannot reach the ear of life in you; but let us talk that we may not feel lonely.

## 42 #

When two women talk they say nothing; when one woman speaks she reveals all of life.

43 #

蛙鳴或許比牛吼宏亮，
但青蛙無法在田裡耕作，
不能轉動酒榨圓輪造酒，
皮囊也無法製成鞋。

43. #

Frogs may bellow louder than bulls, but they cannot
drag the plough in the field not turn the wheel of the
winepress, and of their skins you cannot make shoes.

44 #

僅有啞巴才會豔羨口若懸河之人。

44 #

Only the dumb envy the talkative.

45 #

若冬天說：「春天存在我心。」
有誰相信冬天的話？

45 #

If winter should say, "Spring is in my heart," who would believe winter?

46 #

每顆種子都是份渴求。

46 #

Every seed is a longing.

47 #

若你確實睜眼去看，
就會在眼花撩亂裡看見自己
若你打開耳朵去聽，
就會在眾聲喧嘩中聽見自己。

47 #

Should you really open your eyes and see,
you would behold your image in all images.
And should you open your ears and listen,
you would hear your own voice in all voices.

48 #

發掘真相需要兩個人：
一個述說，一個領悟。

48 #

It takes two of us to discover truth:
one to utter it and one to understand it.

## 49 #

雖然語言的波浪不停拍打在我們身上，
但我們的心底卻永恆不語。

## 50 #

許多教義就像一塊玻璃窗，
我們透過它看見真相，
但它卻讓我們離真相愈來愈遠。

## 51 #

我們來玩捉迷藏吧。
若你藏在我心裡，我就不難找到你。
但若藏在軀殼背後，任誰尋覓都是徒勞。
女人用微笑蒙蔽真實面容。

## 49 #

Though the wave of words is forever upon us, yet our depth is forever silent.

## 50 #

Many a doctrine is like a window pane. We see truth through it but it divides us from truth.

## 51 #

Now let us play hide and seek. Should you hide in my heart it would not be difficult to find you. But should you hide behind your own shell, then it would be useless for anyone to seek you. A woman may veil her face with a smile.

## 52 #

How noble is the sad heart who would sing a joyous song with joyous hearts.

## 53 #

He who would understand a woman, or dissect genius, or solve the mystery of silence is the very man who would wake from a beautiful dream to sit at a breakfast table.

## 54 #

I would walk with all those who walk. I would not stand still to watch the procession passing by.

54 #

我情願跟著所有行進的人前進，
也不愣愣駐望列隊經過。

53 #

可以理解女人，剖析天才，或解決沉默謎團的人，
就是能從美夢甦醒，坐在早餐桌前的那個人。

52 #

一顆悲傷的心能以快樂的心境，
唱出快樂的歌曲，
是件多麼崇高的事啊。

55 #

服侍你的人對你恩重如山。
對他奉獻你的真心，或者換你服侍他。

55 #

You owe more than gold to him who serves you.
Give him of your heart or serve him.

56 #

不，我們沒有白活一場。
他們不是用我們的骨頭蓋了座高塔？

56 #

Nay, we have not lived in vain. Have they not
built towers of our bones?

**57 ＃**

Let us not be particular and sectional.
The poet's mind and the scorpion's tail
rise in glory from the same earth.

**58 ＃**

Every dragon gives birth to a
St. George who slays it.

**57 ＃**

我們切莫斤斤計較，挑三揀四。

詩人的思想與蠍子的尾巴都是從同一塊土地光榮升起。

**58 ＃**

每頭巨龍都誕下一個屠殺自己的聖喬治。

**59 ＃**

樹木是大地在天空寫下的詩詞。

我們砍伐樹木，化為紙張，

好讓我們能記錄自我的空虛。

**59 ＃**

Trees are poems that the earth writes upon the sky. We fell them down and
turn them into paper that we may record our emptiness.

62 #

若一棵樹撰寫自傳，將可能寫出一個種族的歷史。

61 #

他們將筆蘸入我們心底，沾沾自喜他們從中擷取到靈感。

60 #

若你真心想寫作（唯有聖者知道原因），就必須先有知識、藝術與音樂，亦即認識文字的音韻、不矯情的藝術及珍愛讀者的魔法。

## 60 #

Should you care to write (and only the saints know why you should) you must needs have knowledge and art and music -- the knowledge of the music of words, the art of being artless, and the magic of loving your readers.

## 61 #

They dip their pens in our hearts and think they are inspired.

## 62 #

Should a tree write its autobiography it would not be unlike the history of a race.

## 63 #

若我能在落筆寫詩的能力與詩歌想像的狂喜間抉擇，
我會選擇想像，那才是真正的好詩。
但你和我的近鄰無法否認，我的選擇向來錯得離譜。

## 64 #

詩詞不表述想法，而是一首
從淌血傷口或微笑嘴角冉冉升起的歌曲。

## 63 #

If I were to choose between the power of writing a poem and the ecstasy of a
poem unwritten, I would choose the ecstasy. It is better poetry.
But you and all my neighbors agree that I always choose badly.

## 64 #

Poetry is not an opinion expressed. It is a song that rises from a bleeding wound
or a smiling mouth.

65 #

文字永恆不渝。說話與書寫時，要把文字的永恆謹記在心。

65 #

Words are timeless. You should utter them or write them with a knowledge of their timelessness.

66#

詩人是一個罷黜國王，他坐在皇宮的灰燼裡，試圖讓畫面死灰復燃。

66 #

A POET IS a dethroned king sitting among the ashes of his palace trying to fashion an image out of the ashes.

**67 #**

詩詞即是堆積如山的快樂、沉痛與奇蹟，再點綴摻用些許辭海完成。

**68 #**

詩人若尋覓心靈歌曲之母，將是徒勞一場。

**69 #**

我曾對一名詩人說：「在死之前，你的價值我們不會懂。」

他應答：

「死亡向來能揭露真相。

若你真懂我的價值，就知道我的心比我的話語價更高，我的欲望更勝我的手。」

## 67 #

Poetry is a deal of joy and pain and wonder, with a dash of the dictionary.

## 68 #

In vain shall a poet seek the mother of the songs of his heart.

## 69 #

Once I said to a poet, "We shall not know your worth until you die."

And he answered saying, "Yes, death is always the revealer. And if indeed you would know my worth it is that I have more in my heart than upon my tongue, and more in my desire than in my hand."

## 72 #

靈感將永恆歌唱；靈感永遠不需解釋。

## 71 #

詩歌是讓心靈著魔的智慧，智慧是在思想哼唱的詩歌。
若我們能讓人心著魔，同時在他思想裡哼唱，
那他就活在上帝的影子裡。

## 70 #

若你獨自在沙漠之心高歌出美麗，就會獲得聽眾。

## 70 #

If you sing of beauty though alone in the heart of the
desert you will have an audience.

## 71 #

Poetry is wisdom that enchants the heart.
Wisdom is poetry that sings in the mind.
If we could enchant man's heart and at the same time sing in his mind,
Then in truth he would live in the shadow of God.

## 72 #

Inspiration will always sing; inspiration will never explain.

**73 #**

我們太常對孩子唱搖籃曲，唱到連自己都昏昏入睡。

**73 #**

We often sing lullabies to our children that we ourselves may sleep.

**74 #**

所有文字都是自思想盛宴剝落的碎屑。

**74 #**

All our words are but crumbs that fall down from the feast of the mind.

78 #

有言鳴唱愛之歌的夜鶯，胸口必遭荊棘刺穿。

人類亦然，不然我們怎唱？

77 #

若滿嘴食物，你要如何歌唱？

若滿手黃金，怎麼舉手禱告？

76 #

好歌手能唱出我們的沉默。

75 #

思考向來是詩詞的絆腳石。

## 75 #

Thinking is always the stumbling stone to poetry.

## 76 #

A great singer is he who sings our silences.

## 77 #

How can you sing if your mouth be filled with food?

How shall your hand be raised in blessing if it is filled with gold?

## 78 #

They say the nightingale pierces his bosom with a thorn

when he sings his love song.

So do we all. How else should we sing?

## 79 #

Genius is but a robin's song at the beginning of a slow spring.

## 80 #

Even the most winged spirit cannot escape physical necessity.

80 #
即使是背著翅膀的靈魂，
都無法逃離軀殼的需求。

79 #
天才是姍姍來遲的春季展開時，
一首知更鳥的囀調。

83 #
有渴求，就必得滿足。

82 #
靜靜收藏在母親胸懷的那首歌，
會經由她孩子的雙唇哼出調。

81 #
一個狂人與你我一樣，皆是音樂家；
差別在他彈奏的樂器略微走調。

81 #

A madman is not less a musician than you or myself; only the instrument on which he plays is a little out of tune.

82 #

The song that lies silent in the heart of a mother sings upon the lips of her child.

83 #

No longing remains unfulfilled.

84 #

我從未完全認同另一個自我，
事實真理似乎就藏在兩個自我之間。

85 #

你的另一個自我總在自憐，
但另一個自我憑藉悲傷茁壯，
所以剛好互補。

86 #

靈魂與身體不會作繭自縛，
只有靈魂沉睡，身體走調的人，
內心才有掙扎。

84 #

I have never agreed with my other self wholly. The truth of the matter seems to lie between us.

85 #

Your other self is always sorry for you. But your other self grows on sorrow; so all is well.

86 #

There is no struggle of soul and body save in the minds of those whose souls are asleep and whose bodies are out of tune.

87 #

When you reach the heart of life you
shall find beauty in all things, even in
the eyes that are blind to beauty.

88 #

We live only to discover beauty.
All else is a form of waiting.

87 #
當你觸到生命之心，即會發現萬物之美，
即便雙眼對美視而不見亦然。

88 #
我們存在的目的只是為了發掘美，
其餘只是一種等待。

# 89 #

埋下一顆種子，大地會賜予你一朵花。
隨著夢想飛上天，夢就會帶給你所愛。

# 89 #

Sow a seed and the earth will yield you a flower. Dream
your dream to the sky and it will bring you your beloved.

# 90 #

惡魔在你誕辰之日滅亡，
所以你已毋需穿越地獄，才能遇見天使。

# 90 #

The devil died the very day you were born.
Now you do not have to go through hell to meet an angel.

91 #
許多女人短暫租借男人的心；
卻很少女人能擁有一顆真心。

92 #
若你企盼擁有，就切勿索求。

93 #
當男人的手觸到女人的手，
兩人便觸到永恆之心。

## 91 #

Many a woman borrows a man's heart;
very few could possess it.

## 92 #

If you would possess you must not claim.

## 93 #

When a man's hand touches the hand of a woman they both
touch the heart of eternity.

## 94 #

Love is the veil between lover and lover.

## 95 #

Every man loves two women; the one is the creation of
his imagination, and the other is not yet born.

## 96 #

Men who do not forgive women their little faults will never
enjoy their great vitues.

## 96 #

緊捉著女人小惡不放的男人，
將永遠無法享受她們的美德。

## 95 #

每個男人都愛著兩個女人；一個是他
的夢中情人，另一個尚未誕生。

## 94 #

愛情是兩個愛人間的面紗。

97 #
不會隨著每日昇華的愛，
最後變成一種習慣，最終成為奴役。

98 #
愛人擁抱彼此共有的事物，而不是彼此。

99 #
愛情與懷疑永不交談。

## 97 #

Love that does not renew itself every day becomes a habit and in turn a slavery.

## 98 #

Lovers embrace that which is between them rather than each other.

## 99 #

Love and doubt have never been on speaking terms.

## 102 #

若你不能在任何情況下都理解你的朋友，那你就永遠無法懂他。

## 101 #

友誼從來不是機遇，而是甜蜜的負荷。

## 100 #

愛情是一個光的字詞，用光的手，寫在光的頁紙上。

## 100 #

Love is a word of light, written by a hand of light, upon a page of light.

## 101 #

Friendship is always a sweet responsibility, never an opportunity.

## 102 #

If you do not understand your friend under all conditions you will never understand him.

## 103 #

Your most radiant garment is of the other person's weaving;

You most savory meal is that which you eat at the other person's table;

Your most comfortable bed is in the other person's house.

Now tell me, how can you separate yourself from the other person?

## 103 #

你穿過最華麗的外衣是別人縫織而成，

你吃過最美味的一餐來自別人的餐桌，

你睡過最舒適的床鋪亦是別人家裡的。

請告訴我，這樣的你怎能與別人不相往來？

除非你的腦袋不再活在數字裡，
而我的心靈也不再沉淪迷霧中，
否則你的腦袋與我的心靈永遠不會有交集。

104 #

Your mind and my heart will never agree until your mind
ceases to live in numbers and my heart in the mist.

105 #

除非我們將語言減少成七個字，
否則永遠無法理解彼此。

105 #

We shall never understand one another until
we reduce the language to seven words.

106 #

要是不打碎我的心，該怎麼解封？

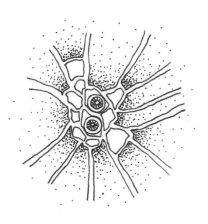

106 #

HOW SHALL MY heart be unsealed unless it be broken?

107 #

Only great sorrow or great joy can reveal your truth.
If you would be revealed you must either dance naked in
the sun, or carry your cross.

107 #

唯有大悲或大喜才能嶄露你的真實。
嶄露自我時，你若非在陽光底下裸舞，
就是扛著一具十字架。

## 109 #

背對太陽，就只能看見自己的影子。

## 108 #

若大自然做到我們所說的滿足，河川就不需尋覓海洋，冬季也不必變成春天。若她做到我們所說的節制，有多少人能享受到這樣的空氣？

## 108 #

Should nature heed what we say of contentment no river would seek the sea, and no winter would turn to Spring. Should she heed all we say of thrift, how many of us would be breathing this air?

## 109 #

You see but your shadow when you turn your back to the sun.

## 110 #

日正當中時，你是自由的；夜晚星空前，你是自由的；

不見太陽、月亮和星辰時，你也是自由的。

不顧世間萬物，合上眼你也是自由的。

唯獨遇到所愛的人，因為你愛他，所以你成了奴隸。

因為他愛你，你便成深愛你的他的奴隸。

## 110 #

You are free before the sun of the day, and free before the stars of the night;

And you are free when there is no sun and no moon and no star.

You are even free when you close your eyes upon all there is.

But you are a slave to him whom you love because you love him,

And a slave to him who loves you because he loves you.

## 111 #

We are all beggars at the gate of the temple, and each one of us receives his share of the bounty of the King when he enters the temple, and when he goes out.
But we are all jealous of one another, which is another way of belittling the King.

## 112 #

You cannot consume beyond your appetite. The other half of the loaf belongs to the other person, and there should remain a little bread for the chance guest.

## 112 #

你不能過食，那半條麵包是別人的，
此外也該留點麵包給意想不到的客人。

## 111 #

皇宮大門前的我們皆乞丐，
國王進出宮時，人人都能獲得他的賞賜，
然我們卻彼此嫉妒，等於對國王輕蔑。

113 #

要不是客人造訪，
你們所有的房屋都僅是墳墓。

113 #

If it were not for your guests all houses would be graves.

114 #

殷勤的野狼對單純的羊說：
「不知您們願意賞光，造訪寒舍？」
羊回答道：
「若您們無意將我們吞下肚，當樂意造訪。」

114 #

Said a gracious wolf to a simple sheep, "Will you not honor our house with a visit?"
And the sheep answered, "We would have been honored to visit your house if it were not in your stomach."

## 115 #

我在門檻前攔下客人，道：

「不，進門前毋需擦腳，離開時擦腳即可。」

## 116 #

慷慨並非將我需要之物施予我，而是將你更需要之物贈與我。

## 117 #

施予讓人寬厚慷慨，但在施予同時，記得把臉轉開，才不會看見受者的羞赧。

## 115 #

I stopped my guest on the threshold and said, "Nay, wipe not your feet as you enter, but as you go out."

## 116 #

Generosity is not in giving me that which I need more than you do, but it is in giving me that which you need more than I do.

## 117 #

You are indeed charitable when you give, and while giving, turn your face away so that you may not see the shyness of the receiver.

120 #

天使與惡魔也探視過我，但我擺脫了他們。

天使造訪時，我如往昔一般禱告，他便感無聊。

惡魔光臨時，我犯下已犯過的罪過，他也走開了。

119 #

人常與明天借貸，好償還昨日債務。

118 #

窮人與富人間的差距，

只有一日的飢餓與一小時的乾渴。

## 118 #

The difference between the richest man and the poorest is but a day of hunger
and an hour of thirst.

## 119 #

We often borrow from our tomorrows to pay our debts to our yesterdays.

## 120 #

I too am visited by angels and devils, but I get rid of them.

When it is an angel I pray an old prayer, and he is bored;

When it is a devil I commit an old sin, and he passes me by.

## 121 #

這座監獄說來不差，但我不滿牢房與鄰房獄友間的牆；
但我向你保證，我絕不是責備獄卒，也不怪罪監獄建工。

## 122 #

聽到你要一隻魚，卻給你一條蛇的人，
或許除了蛇便別無他物，已可謂慷慨。

## 123 #

詭計偶爾奏效，卻必自尋死路。

## 121 #

After all this is not a bad prison; but I do not like this wall
between my cell and the next prisoner's cell;
Yet I assure you that I do not wish to reproach the warder not
the Builder of the prison.

## 122 #

Those who give you a serpent when you ask for a fish, may have
nothing but serpents to give. It is then generosity on their part.

## 123 #

Trickery succeeds sometimes, but it always commits suicide.

126 #
怎能冀盼花兒在你手心綻放？
若你的心猶如一座火山，

125 #
就是有資格觸碰上帝衣襬的人。
真正有資格區別好壞善惡之人，

124 #
還真是大肚能容。
誓死不偷的竊賊、只說實話的騙徒，
若你原諒滴血不濺的殺人犯、

## 124 #

You are truly a forgiver when you forgive murderers who never spill blood, thieves who never steal, and liars who utter no falsehood.

## 125 #

He who can put his finger upon that which divides good from evil is he who can touch the very hem of the garment of God.

## 126 #

If your heart is a volcano how shall you expect flowers to bloom in your hands?

# 127 #

A strange form of self-indulgence! There are times when I would be wronged and cheated, that I may laugh at the expense of those who think I do not know I am being wronged and cheated.

# 128 #

What shall I say of him who is the pursuer playing the part of the pursued?

# 129 #

Let him who wipes his soiled hands with your garment take your garment. He may need it again; surely you would not.

## 129 #

若有人把骯髒雙手抹在你衣衫上，把衣衫送他吧，

他可能還需要衣服，你肯定已不需要。

## 128 #

追人者，卻假裝自己遭到追趕，

面對這樣的人，我有什麼好說？

## 127 #

多麼奇怪的自欺欺人啊！

有時我寧可受欺騙虧待，

再放聲嘲笑那些以為我不自知受騙虧待的人。

131 #

切勿利用後天習得的美德，洗白你固有的缺陷。我願擁戴缺陷；缺陷是我的一部分。

130 #

真遺憾，兌錢商不可能成為好園丁。

## 130 #

It is a pity that money-changers cannot be good gardeners.

## 131 #

Please do not whitewash your inherent faults with your acquired virtues. I would have the faults; they are like mine own.

## 132 #

How often have I attributed to myself crimes I have never committed, so that the other person may feel comfortable in my presence.

## 133 #

Even the masks of life are masks of deeper mystery.

133 #
就連生命的面具，都是張更深奧的神秘面罩。

132 #
為了讓他人在我面前自在，我常承擔不是我造就的罪。

136 #
唯有愚夫與天才破壞人為法則；
他們是最接近上帝之心的人。

135 #
想分擔你犯下的罪的，才是真正公義之人。

134 #
你或許會只憑自己的認知，批判他者。
說吧，你認為我們之中誰有罪？誰又無罪？

134 #

You may judge others only according to your knowledge of yourself.
Tell me now, who among us is guilty and who is unguilty?

135 #

The truly just is he who feels half guilty of your misdeeds.

136 #

Only an idiot and a genius break man-made laws; and
they are the nearest to the heart of God.

139 #
你與敵人臨終在即時，將握手言和。

138 #
神啊，我沒有敵人，若要賜給我一個敵人，
請賦予他與我匹敵的力量，並僅讓真理得勝。

137 #
背後有人追逐，你才會健步如飛。

## 137 #

It is only when you are pursued that you become swift.

## 138 #

I have no enemies, O God, but if I am to have an enemy

Let his strength be equal to mine,

That truth alone may be the victor.

## 139 #

You will be quite friendly with your enemy when you both die.

很久以前，有個慈愛又人見人愛的男人，被釘死在十字架上。

說也奇怪，我昨天遇見他三回。

第一回，他拜託警察切勿送一名妓女入獄。

第二回，他跟一名流浪漢飲酒。

第三回，他在教堂裡與一名執事大打出手。

一個人也許會為了自保而自盡。

## 140 #

Perhaps a man may commit suicide in self-defense.

## 141 #

Long ago there lived a Man who was crucified for being too loving and too lovable.
And strange to relate I met him thrice yesterday.
The first time He was asking a policeman not to take a prostitute to prison; the second time He was drinking wine with an outcast; and the third time He was having a fistfight with a promoter inside a church.

## 142 #

If all they say of good and evil were true, then my life is but one long crime.

## 143 #

Pity is but half justice.

## 144 #

THE ONLY ONE who has been unjust to me is the one to whose brother I have been unjust.

144 #
唯一對我不公不義的人，
他的兄弟曾受我不公不義對待。

143 #
憐憫只做到一半的公義。

142 #
若他們所說的善惡皆為真，
那我的人生就是串漫長的罪惡清單。

## 146 #

我時常痛恨自我辯駁；

然若我更堅強，又怎需動用這般武器。

## 145 #

見到一個男人被帶入監獄，請在內心默想：

「或許他將送進一間更寬敞的監獄。」

遇見一個醉醺醺的男人，請在內心默想：

「或許他逃離某個更不美麗的世界。」

## 145 #

When you see a man led to prison say in your heart, "Mayhap he is escaping from a narrower prison."

And when you see a man drunken say in your heart, "Mayhap he sought escape from something still more unbeautiful."

## 146 #

Oftentimes I have hated in self-defense; but if I were stronger I would not have used such a weapon.

147 #

How stupid is he who would patch the hatred in
his eyes with the smile of his lips.

147 #
利用唇邊笑意彌補眼底恨意，
是多麼愚蠢的事啊。

148 #

唯在我之下者，有資格對我嫉妒怨懟，
但從未有人嫉妒怨懟我；沒人比我卑微。
唯在我之上者，有資格對我讚許輕蔑，
但從未有人讚許輕蔑我；沒人凌駕於我。

148 #

Only those beneath me can envy or hate me.

I have never been envied nor hated; I am above no one.

Only those above me can praise or belittle me.

I have never been praised nor belittled; I am below no one.

151 #

你憐憫動作遲緩之人，而非思想駑鈍者，
同情眼瞎之人，而非心盲者，真是怪哉。

150 #

也不比預言家低。
會發現自己的地位既不比重罪犯高，
當你找到生命核心，

149 #

你對我說：「我不了解你，」
這句話是高估我的讚美，也是你不應得的屈辱。
當人生賜予我黃金，我施你銀子，
此舉何等卑劣，我卻自認慷慨。

## 149 #

Your saying to me, "I do not understand you," is praise beyond my worth, and
an insult you do not deserve. How mean am I when life gives me gold and I give
you silver, and yet I deem myself generous.

## 150 #

When you reach the heart of life you will find yourself not higher than the
felon, and not lower than the prophet.

## 151 #

Strange that you should pity the slow-footed and not the slow-minded,
And the blind-eyed rather than the blind-hearted.

## 152 #

It is wiser for the lame not to break his crutches upon the head of his enemy.

## 153 #

How blind is he who gives you out of his pocket that he may take out of your heart.

## 154 #

Life is a procession. The slow of foot finds it too swift and he steps out;
And the swift of foot finds it too slow and he too steps out.

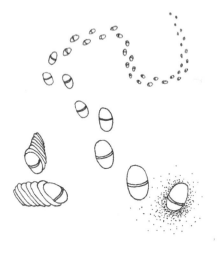

### 154 #

人生是一列行進隊伍。

腳步悠悠者覺得過於迅速，於是離開；

行色匆匆者認為太過緩慢，於是也離開。

### 153 #

他以為從自己口袋掏東西給你，

就能贏得你心，真是盲目。

### 152 #

瘸子不高舉拐杖，毆打敵人腦袋，此乃明智之舉。

## 157 #

人人皆為階下囚，只是有些人的牢房有窗，有些人的沒窗。

## 156 #

真正的好人，是與大家公認的壞人並肩同在者。

## 155 #

若真有罪孽，有些人跟隨先人，重蹈覆轍，犯了退步的罪；
有些人威壓後輩，咄咄逼人，犯了踰矩的罪。

## 155 #

If there is such a thing as sin some of us commit it backward following our
forefathers' footsteps;
And some of us commit it forward by overruling our children.

## 156 #

The truly good is he who is one with all those who are deemed bad.

## 157 #

We are all prisoners but some of us are in cells with windows and some without.

## 158 #

Strange that we all defend our wrongs with more vigor than we do our rights.

## 159 #

Should we all confess our sins to one another we would all laugh at one another for our lack of originality.

Should we all reveal our virtues we would also laugh for the same cause.

## 160 #

An individual is above man-made laws until he commits a crime against man-made conventions; After that he is neither above anyone nor lower than anyone.

160 #

除非違背人為常規，否則人高於人為律法；犯了罪之後，他就既不高於任何人，也不低於任何人。

159 #

若我們彼此坦誠罪惡，就會自嘲沒創意。

若我們彼此展現美德，也會自嘲老掉牙。

158 #

我們犯錯時的狡辯，居然比爭取權利時洪亮，真是奇怪。

# 161 #

Government is an agreement between you and myself.
You and myself are often wrong.

# 162 #

Crime is either another name of need or
an aspect of a disease.

# 163 #

Is there a greater fault than being conscious
of the other person's faults?

161 #

政府是你我之間的協定，然而你我卻往往大錯特錯。

162 #

犯罪若非需求的別名，就是疾病的同類。

163 #

還有比意識到他人缺點更嚴重的缺點嗎？

## 164 #

別人嘲笑你，你可以同情他；你嘲笑他人，卻可能無法原諒自己。

別人傷害你，你可以卻忘傷害；你傷害他人，卻將永遠無法釋懷。

其實他人就是你最纖細敏感的自我，只是換了一具軀體。

## 165 #

你要人戴著你的翅膀飛翔，卻連羽毛都不肯給他們，難道不是有口無心。

## 164 #

If the other person laughs at you, you can pity him; but if you laugh at him you may never forgive yourself.

If the other person injures you, you may forget the injury; but if you injure him you will always remember.

In truth the other person is your most sensitive self given another body.

## 165 #

How heedless you are when you would have men fly with your wings and you cannot even give them a feather.

沙與沫 Sand and Foam

## 168 #

遇害者的光榮，就是他不是殺人兇手。

## 167 #

仇恨是死透的。你們誰想當墳墓？

## 166 #

有個男人坐在我桌前，
吃了我的麵包，喝我的葡萄酒，卻訕笑著離去。
待他再回來討麵包與葡萄酒，我將他逐出門外；
這會兒便換天使嘲笑我。

## 166 #

Once a man sat at my board and ate my bread and drank my wine and went away
laughing at me.
Then he came again for bread and wine, and I spurned him;
And the angels laughed at me.

## 167 #

Hate is a dead thing. Who of you would be a tomb?

## 168 #

It is the honor of the murdered that he is not the murderer.

**169 #**

人性的護民官，存於它沉默不語的心底，
而不是大談闊論的思想。

**170 #**

我不販賣我的時光換取黃金，他們認為我是瘋子；
而他們認為我的時光可販售，我認為他們是瘋子。

**171 #**

他們在我們面前攤開黃金銀兩、象牙黑檀，
我們在他們面前掏出我們的真心與靈魂；
他們卻認為自己是主，我們是客。

**169 #**

The tribune of humanity is in its silent heart, never its talkative mind.

**170 #**

They deem me mad because I will not sell my days for gold;

And I deem them mad because they think my days have a price.

**171 #**

They spread before us their riches of gold and silver, of ivory and ebony, and we

spread before them our hearts and our spirits.;

And yet they deem themselves the hosts and us the guests.

## 172 #

I would not be the least among men with dreams and the desire to fulfill them, rather than the greatest with no dreams and no desires.

## 172 #

我寧願當一個渴望實踐夢想的小人物，也不願是個不懷抱夢想、無欲無求的偉人。

## 173 #

最可悲的人就是把夢想寄託在金銀財寶的人。

## 173 #

The most pitiful among men is he who turns his dreams into silver and gold.

176 #

我不會聆聽一名征服者對征服對象說教。

175 #

若不知曉，就切勿對人妄下評斷，你知道的是那麼有限啊。

174 #

我們正努力攀上內心想望的高峰。

若他人竊走你的行囊與錢財，耗用你的財物，增加自我重量，你要憐憫他；

他的身體更難負荷攀登，重擔讓路途更加漫長。

看見他氣喘吁吁往上爬，身輕如燕的你拉他一把吧；這對你的速度有幫助。

## 174 #

We are all climbing toward the summit of our hearts' desire. Should the other climber steal your sack and your purse and wax fat on the one and heavy on the other, you should pity him;

The climbing will be harder for his flesh, and the burden will make his way longer. And should you in your leanness see his flesh puffing upward, help him a step; it will add to your swiftness.

## 175 #

You cannot judge any man beyond your knowledge of him, and how small is your knowledge.

## 176 #

I would not listen to a conqueror preaching to the conquered.

## 177 #

The truly free man is he who bears the load of the bond slave patiently.

## 178 #

A thousand years ago my neighbor said to me, "I hate life, for it is naught but a thing of pain."

And yesterday I passed by a cemetery and saw life dancing upon his grave.

## 179 #

Strife in nature is but disorder longing for order.

## 179 #

大自然的紛亂衝突，不過是渴望秩序的失序。

## 178 #

一千年前，鄰居對我說：
「我恨人生，人生只帶來疼痛，一無是處。」
昨日我行經墓地，發現人生在他的墓上翩然起舞。

## 177 #

真正自由之人能堅忍扛起奴隸的重擔。

Solitude is a silent storm that breaks down all
our dead branches;
Yet it sends our living roots deeper into the
living heart of the living earth.

181 #

180 #

孤寂是場折斷我們枯枝的寂靜暴風；
卻讓我們的生命之根，深深扎入生氣勃勃大地的生命核心。

181 #

我曾對溪水訴說大海，溪水當我在誇大幻想；
我曾對大海訴說溪水，大海當我是輕蔑毀謗。

181 #

Once I spoke of the sea to a brook, and the brook thought me but
an imaginative exaggerator;
And once I spoke of a brook to the sea, and the sea thought me
but a depreciative defamer.

184 #

深長者垂直探入深處，高聳者筆直拔高升天；唯獨遼闊無邊才能自在遨遊。

183 #

在這裡獲得最高讚揚的美德，在他處卻可能最微不足道。

182 #

讚頌螞蟻的庸碌，卻輕貶蚱蜢的歌聲，眼界多麼狹隘啊。

## 182 #

How narrow is the vision that exalts the busyness of the ant above the singing of the grasshopper.

## 183 #

The highest virtue here may be the least in another world.

## 184 #

The deep and the high go to the depth or to the height in a straight line; only the spacious can move in circles.

## 185 #

IF IT WERE not for our conception of weights and measures we would stand in awe of the firefly as we do before the sun.

## 186 #

A scientist without imagination is a butcher with dull knives and out-worn scales. But what would you, since we are not all vegetarians?

## 187 #

When you sing the hungry hears you with his stomach.

185 #

若非重量與尺度，我們就會猶如敬畏太陽，對螢火蟲敬畏三分。

186 #

不具想像力的科學家，就是刀鈍秤斜的屠夫。既然我們並非都吃素，你能怎麼做？

187 #

你高歌時，飢餓的人就用他的空胃聽。

190 #

或許人類的喪禮，就是天使的婚宴。

189 #

若你非要直言不諱，就說得動聽些；否則就保持沉默，因為鄰人正漸漸死亡。

188 #

跟新生兒相比，老人與死亡的距離並無更近；生命亦同。

## 188 #

Death is not nearer to the aged than to the new-born; neither is life.

## 189 #

If indeed you must be candid, be candid beautifully; otherwise keep silent, for there is a man in our neighborhood who is dying.

## 190 #

Mayhap a funeral among men is a wedding feast among the angels.

# 191 #

A forgotten reality may die and leave in its will
seven thousand actualities and facts to be spent
in its funeral and the building of a tomb.

# 191 #

遭到遺忘的現實可能死去，留下遺囑，
裡頭寫滿七千條用於喪禮與掘墓的事實與真相。

# 192 #

In truth we talk only to ourselves, but sometimes
we talk loud enough that others may hear us.

# 192 #

我們只對自己說真話，
但有時嗓門可能響到被別人聽見。

195 #
除非我是醫師中的醫師，否則他們不相信我是天文學家。

194 #
若銀河不存在我心底，我是怎麼看見或認識它的？

193 #
除非有人平鋪直述說出口，否則我們視而不見明顯事實。

193 #

The obvious is that which is never seen until someone expresses it simply.

194 #

If the Milky Way were not within me how should I have seen it or known it?

195 #

Unless I am a physician among physicians they would not believe that I am an astronomer.

## 196 #

Perhaps the sea's definition of a shell is the pearl.
Perhaps time's definition of coal is the diamond.

## 197 #

Fame is the shadow of passion standing in the light.

## 198 #

A root is a flower that disdains fame.

## 198 #

根是一朵蔑視名氣的花。

## 197 #

名氣是熱情立在光裡的陰影。

## 196 #

也許海洋對貝殼的定義是珍珠。
也許時間對煤炭的定義是鑽石。

201 #
真正偉大的人，既非誰的主人，也不是誰的僕人。

200 #
我所知道的偉大之人，他們的性格都有渺小之處；正是這種渺小，讓他們不至於放棄、發狂或自盡。

199 #
美之外，既無宗教，也無科學。

## 199 #

There is neither religion nor science beyond beauty.

## 200 #

Every great man I have known had something small in his make-up; and it was that small something which prevented inactivity or madness or suicide.

## 201 #

The truly great man is he who would master no one, and who would be mastered by none.

## 202 #

I would not believe that a man is mediocre simply because he kills the criminals and the prophets.

## 203 #

Tolerance is love sick with the sickness of haughtiness.

## 204 #

Worms will turn; but is it not strange that even elephants will yield?

## 204 #

蠕蟲會彎曲；但就連大象都會屈服，你說奇不奇怪？

## 203 #

容忍對傲慢病犯了相思。

## 202 #

我不相信一個人只因殺了罪犯和預言家，就是平庸之輩。

207 #

我們都在尋覓聖山巔峰；但我們若能把過去當作地圖，而非嚮導，這條路線不是更短？

206 #

我既是火焰，也是乾木叢，某一個我吞噬掉另一個我。

205 #

爭執是兩種思想間最短的捷徑。

## 205 #

A disagreement may be the shortest cut between two minds.

## 206 #

I am the flame and I am the dry bush, and one part of me consumes the other part.

## 207 #

We are all seeking the summit of the holy moutain; but shall not our road be shorter if we consider the past a chart and not a guide?

## 208 #

Wisdom ceases to be wisdom when it becomes too proud to weep, too grave to laugh, and too self-ful to seek other than itself.

## 209 #

Had I filled myself with all that you know what room should I have for all that you do not know?

## 210 #

I have learned silence from the talkative, toleration from the intolerant, and kindness from the unkind; yet strange, I am ungrateful to these teachers.

## 208 #

智慧要是驕傲到不願流淚，嚴肅到無法大笑，自以為是到不求助於人，便不再是智慧。

## 209 #

我若用你知道的一切填滿自己，還有空間容納你不知的一切嗎？

## 210 #

我從侃侃而談的人身上學會沉默，向不知容忍者學會包容，向刻薄無情者學會善良；奇怪的是，我卻對這些老師毫無感激之情。

## 214 #

誇大即是勃然大怒的真相。

## 213 #

當你抵達知識的尾聲，就是感受的開始。

## 212 #

善妒者的沉默喧囂沸騰。

## 211 #

冥頑不靈的人總愛強詞奪理。

## 211 #

A bigot is a stone-leaf orator.

## 212 #

The silence of the envious is too noisy.

## 213 #

When you reach the end of what you should know, you will be at the beginning of what you should sense.

## 214 #

An exaggeration is a truth that has lost its temper.

## 215 #

If you can see only what light reveals and hear only what sound announces,
Then in truth you do not see nor do you hear.

## 216 #

A fact is a truth unsexed.

## 217 #

You cannot laugh and be unkind at the same time.

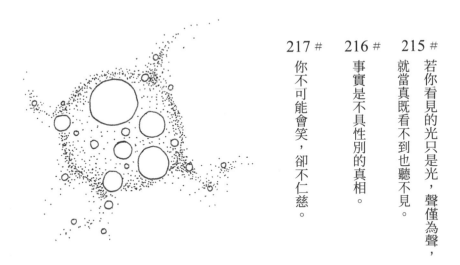

## 217 #

你不可能會笑，卻不仁慈。

## 216 #

事實是不具性別的真相。

## 215 #

若你看見的光只是光，聲僅為聲，
就當真既看不到也聽不見。

220 #
在任一塊土地挖掘，都能挖到寶藏，重點是必須帶著農夫的信念去掘。

219 #
羞慚的失敗比不知謙遜的成功高尚。

218 #
最得我心的，是一個沒有王國的國王，及不知乞討的窮人。

218 #

The nearest to my heart are a king without a kingdom and a poor man who does not know how to beg.

219 #

A shy failure is nobler than an immodest success.

220 #

Dig anywhere in the earth and you will find a treasure, only you must dig with the faith of a peasant.

## 221 #

Said a hunted fox followed by twenty horsemen and a pack of twenty hounds,
"Of course they will kill me. But how poor and how stupid they must be.
Surely it would not be worth while for twenty foxes riding on twenty asses and
accompanied by twenty wolves to chase and kill one man."

## 222 #

It is the mind in us that yields to the laws made by us, but never the spirit in us.

## 221 #

一隻狐狸遭率領二十隻獵犬的二十個騎兵獵捕，他說：

「他們當然會殺了我，但他們多傻多可憐啊。

想想二十隻狐狸騎著二十頭驢，率領二十頭狼，

只為追殺一個人，怎可能值得。」

## 222 #

我們的思想屈服於人為制定的法規，

但我們的心靈卻從未讓步。

225 #
生命提高音量：「現在你聽見我了。」
我對生命說：「我想聽死亡說話。」

224 #
一個女人高聲抗議：
「這當然是場正義之戰，我兒子為此殞落。」

223 #
我是旅人，亦是航海家，
每天都在我的靈魂裡發現新大陸。

## 223 #

A traveler am I and a navigator, and every day I discover a new region within my soul.

## 224 #

A woman protested saying, "Of course it was a righteous war. My son fell in it."

## 225 #

I said to Life, "I would hear Death speak."
And Life raised her voice a little higher and said, "You hear him now."

## 226 #

When you have solved all the mysteries of life you long for death, for it is but another mystery of life.

## 227 #

Birth and death are the two noblest expressions of bravery.

227 #

出生與死亡是兩種最高尚的英勇展現。

226 #

等到你解出生命的所有祕密，便會渴望死亡，因為死亡是生命另一個祕密。

## 228 #

朋友啊，你我與生命，與彼此，與自己應形同陌路，

除非哪天你開口，而我傾聽，能夠認定你的聲音就是我的；

當我站在你跟前，我也能以為自己就站在鏡子前。

## 229 #

他們對我說：

「你認識了自己，就等於認識了所有人。」

我則說：「除非我接觸所有人，否則不會認識自己。」

## 230 #

一個人有兩面；

其中一個在黑暗中清醒，另一個在光明裡沉睡。

## 228 #

My friend, you and I shall remain strangers unto life,

And unto one another, and each unto himself,

Until the day when you shall speak and I shall listen

Deeming your voice my own voice;

And when I shall stand before you

Thinking myself standing before a mirror.

## 229 #

They say to me, "Should you know yourself you would know all men."

And I say, "Only when I seek all men shall I know myself."

## 230 #

MAN IS TWO men; one is awake in darkness, the other is asleep in light.

## 231 #

A hermit is one who renounces the world of fragments that he may enjoy
the world wholly and without interruption.

## 232 #

There lies a green field between the scholar and the poet; should the scholar
cross it he becomes a wise man; should the poet cross it, he becomes a prophet.

## 232 #

學者與詩人間存在一片綠地；
學者跨越那片綠地，就成了智者；
詩人跨越那片綠地，則成為預言家。

## 231 #

隱者退出碎片斑駁的世界，
這樣才可不受干擾，完整享受這個世界。

233 #

Yestereve I saw philosophers in the market-place carrying their heads in baskets, and crying aloud, "Wisdom! Wisdom for sale!"

Poor philosophers! They must needs sell their heads to feed their hearts. Said a philosopher to a street sweeper, "I pity you. Yours is a hard and dirty task."

And the street sweeper said, "Thank you, sir. But tell me what is your task?"

And the philosopher answered saying, "I study man's mind, his deeds and his desires."

Then the street sweeper went on with his sweeping and said with a smile, "I pity you too."

233 #

昨夜我在市集碰到一群哲學家，手裡拎裝著自己頭顱的籃子，

叫賣：「智慧！智慧！來買智慧！」

可憐的哲學家！

他們得出賣自己的頭，才得以餵養自我的心。

有位哲學家對掃街清潔工說：

「我同情你。你的工作艱辛又骯髒。」

掃街清潔工回道：

「先生，謝謝您。敢問您從事哪行？」

哲學家應答：

「我研究人類的思想、行為和欲望。」

清潔工繼續打掃，嘴角帶著笑意：

「我也同情你。」

234 #

聆聽真相的人，並不比說出真相的人差。

235 #

沒人能在必要與奢侈間畫出分界線，唯有天使能辦到，天使聰慧而深思熟慮。

也許天使是我們遠在太空裡的清晰思想。

234 #

He who listens to truth is not less than he who utters truth.

235 #

No man can draw the line between necessities and luxuries. Only the angels can do that, and the angels are wise and wistful.

Perhaps the angels are our better thought in space.

239 #　238 #　237 #　236 #

過往的人現皆與我們共居，想當然沒人想當怠慢的主人。

事實上你並不虧欠任何人，你只是虧欠所有人。

慷慨就是賦予你所不能予，自尊就是不接受你所需。

在苦行僧心底找到王位，即是真正的王子。

## 236 #

He is the true prince who finds his throne in the heart of the dervish.

## 237 #

Generosity is giving more than you can, and pride is taking less than you need.

## 238 #

In truth you owe naught to any man. You owe all to all men.

## 239 #

All those who have lived in the past live with us now. Surely none of us would be an ungracious host.

240 #

最多渴望的人，活得最長久。

241 #

他們對我說：「一鳥在手，勝過十鳥在林。」
我卻道：「一鳥一羽在林，勝過十鳥在手。」
你對羽毛的追尋，是在追尋擁有羽翼雙足的生命；
不，是生命本身。

242 #

世上僅有兩種元素，美與真理；
美存於情人心底，真理則在耕者手裡。

## 240 #

He who longs the most lives the longest.

## 241 #

They say to me, "A bird in the hand is worth
ten in the bush."
But I say, "A bird and a feather in the bush is
worth more than ten birds in the hand."
Your seeking after that feather is life with
winged feet; nay, it is life itself.

## 242 #

There are only two elements here, beauty and
truth; beauty in the hearts of lovers, and truth
in the arms of the tillers of the soil.

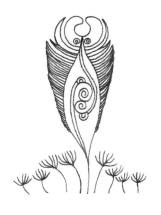

245 #

我景仰對我吐露思想的人；我尊敬對我傾訴夢想的人。
但為何我在服侍我的人面前如此害羞，甚至略感羞愧？

244 #

比起能眼見為憑的人，
在殷殷盼望的人心底，美更閃爍明艷。

243 #

偉大之美擄獲我心，但更偉大的美讓我從中獲得解放。

243 #

Great beauty captures me, but a beauty still greater frees me even from itself.

244 #

Beauty shines brighter in the heart of him who longs for it than in the eyes of him who sees it.

245 #

I admire him who reveals his mind to me; I honor him who unveils his dreams. But why am I shy, and even a little ashamed before him who serves me?

## 248 #

智慧通常是張面具，若你能拆穿它，
就會發現一個惱怒的天才，或者耍花招的小聰明。

## 247 #

天使知道有太多實際的人，
一邊帶著夢想家的面目流汗，一邊吃著麵包。

## 246 #

才子曾以服侍王子為榮，
現在則以服務貧民為傲。

## 246 #

The gifted were once proud in serving princes.
Now they claim honor in serving paupers.

## 247 #

The angels know that too many practical men eat their bread with the sweat of
the dreamer's brow.

## 248 #

Wit is often a mask. If you could tear it you would find either a genius irritated
or cleverness juggling.

251 #
將失去通往天堂七扇門的鑰匙。
與你一起享福，卻不能共度難關的人，

250 #
才能推敲出我們內心的祕密。
唯獨內心藏有祕密的人，

249 #
我想這兩者都沒說錯。
聰明的人認為我聰明，愚鈍的人覺得我愚鈍。

249 #

The understanding attributes to me understanding and the dull, dullness. I think they are both right.

250 #

Only those with secrets in their hearts could divine the secrets in our hearts.

251 #

He who would share your pleasure but not your pain shall lose the key to one of the seven gates of Paradise.

253 #

我們早在體會快樂與悲傷前，選擇了快樂與悲傷。

252 #

極樂世界確實存在；它就在帶領群羊踏上綠地，哄孩子入眠，抒發最後一行詩句裡。

## 252 #

Yes, there is a Nirvanah; it is in leading your sheep to a green pasture, and in putting your child to sleep, and in writing the last line of your poem.

## 253 #

We choose our joys and our sorrows long before we experience them.

254 #

哀傷僅是兩座花園間的一堵牆。

255 #

當你的快樂或憂愁壯大，世界就變得渺小。

256 #

欲望是半條生命；冷漠則是半份死亡。

254 #

Sadness is but a wall between two gardens.

255 #

When either your joy or your sorrow becomes great the world becomes small.

256 #

Desire is half of life; idifference is half of death.

## 259 #

信念就是人心裡的一片綠洲，
思想的商隊則從來無法到達。

## 258 #

他們對我說：

「你必須在今世的喜悅與來世的平靜間做抉擇。」

我對他們說：

「我已經選擇了今世的快樂與來世的平靜，

因為我內心知曉，至高詩人只寫一首詩，

這首詩的格律完美，韻腳也完美。」

## 257 #

今日的哀傷，最苦澀的莫過於昨日喜悅的回憶。

## 257 #

The bitterest thing in our today's sorrow is the memory of our yesterday's joy.

## 258 #

They say to me, "You must needs choose between the pleasures of this world and the peace of the next world."

And I say to them, "I have chosen both the delights of this world and the peace of the next. For I know in my heart that the Supreme Poet wrote but one poem, and it scans perfectly, and it also rhymes perfectly."

## 259 #

Faith is an oasis in the heart which will never be reached by the caravan of thinking.

262 #

春季花蕊是天使在早餐桌上訴說的冬季美夢。

261 #

若你對風傾訴祕密，莫怪風洩露予樹。

260 #

登上巔峰後，你只會為了欲求而欲求；只為飢餓而飢餓；為更多渴望而渴望。

## 260 #

When you reach your height you shall desire but only for desire; and you shall hunger, for hunger; and you shall thirst for greater thirst.

## 261 #

If you reveal your secrets to the wind you should not blame the wind for revealing them to the trees.

## 262 #

The flowers of spring are winter's dreams related at the breakfast table of the angels.

263 #

Said a skunk to a tube-rose, "See how swiftly I run, while you cannot walk nor even creep."

Said the tube-rose to the skunk, "Oh, most noble swift runner, please run swiftly!"

264 #

Turtles can tell more about roads than hares.

265 #

Strange that creatures without backbones have the hardest shells.

263 #

一隻臭鼬對一朵晚香玉說：

「瞧我健步如飛，你卻連走或爬都不會。」

晚香玉對臭鼬說：

「噢，高尚的飛毛腿，我請你快跑吧！」

264 #

烏龜對道路的了解遠勝於野兔。

265 #

怪哉，不具脊骨的動物，居然擁有最堅硬的外殼。

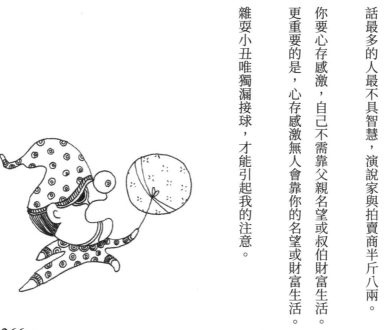

268 #
雜耍小丑唯獨漏接球，才能引起我的注意。

267 #
你要心存感激，自己不需靠父親名望或叔伯財富生活。
更重要的是，心存感激無人會靠你的名望或財富生活。

266 #
話最多的人最不具智慧，演說家與拍賣商半斤八兩。

## 266 #

The most talkative is the least intelligent, and there is hardly a difference between an orator and an auctioneer.

## 267 #

Be grateful that you do not have to live down the renown of a father nor the wealth of an uncle.
But above all be grateful that no one will have to live down either your renown or your wealth.

## 268 #

Only when a juggler misses catching his ball does he appeal to me.

# 269 #

The envious praises me unknowingly.

# 270 #

Long were you a dream in your mother's sleep, and then she woke to give you birth.

# 271 #

The germ of the race is in your mother's longing.

## 269 #

心存嫉妒者在不知不覺間誇讚了我。

## 270 #

你是母親睡眠中一場漫長的夢，她醒來後誕下了你。

## 271 #

種族的萌芽就在你母親的渴求裡。

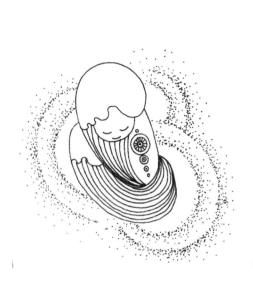

273 #

我們誕下的孩子有些理所當然，有些令人懊悔。

272 #

我的雙親渴望一個孩子，於是有了我。

我渴望雙親，於是有了夜與海。

## 272 #

My father and mother desired a child and they begot me.

And I wanted a mother and a father and I begot night and the sea.

## 273 #

Some of our children are our justifications and some are but our regrets.

274 #

當夜幕低垂，你是一片黑暗，認真仰躺休息。

當白晝來臨，你仍一片漆黑，起身時起勁地對白日說：「我仍黑暗。」

對黑夜白晝裝腔作勢乃愚笨之舉，它們只會恥笑你。

275 #

迷霧繚繞裡的高山不是小丘；

細雨紛飛中的橡樹亦非垂柳。

276 #

真矛盾啊：比起高度居中的兩者，

高聳深長者之間的距離更近。

274 #

When night comes and you too are dark, lie down and be dark with a will.

And when morning comes and you are still dark stand up and say to the day with a will, "I am still dark."

It is stupid to play a role with the night and the day.
They would both laugh at you.

275 #

The mountain veiled in mist is not a hill; an oak tree in the rain is not a weeping willow.

276 #

Behold here is a paradox; the deep and high are nearer to one another than the mid-level to either.

279 #

若愛沒有持續茁壯，便在不斷衰亡。

278 #

當你以愛鄰為樂，這便不再是美德了。

277 #

若我是佇立你眼前的一面明鏡，
你望入我，瞥見自我容顏，然後說：「我愛你，」
實際上你只是愛著我反射出的你。

## 277 #

When I stood a clear mirror before you, you gazed into me and saw your image.

Then you said, "I love you."

But in truth you loved yourself in me.

## 278 #

When you enjoy loving your neighbor it ceases to be a virtue.

## 279 #

Love which is not always springing is always dying.

你不可能年輕，同時意識到年輕；

年輕忙著生活而不自知，意識則忙尋覓年輕而忘卻生活。

你坐在窗邊觀看行人，

目睹一名修女走向你的右手邊，一名娼妓走向左手邊，

也許會無知地說道：

「她是如此聖潔啊，而她是那麼卑賤。」

但閉上雙眼聆聽，就會聽見空氣中飄著細語：

「有人帶著禱告來找我，有人帶著傷痛去看她，

她倆的靈魂中，都有我靈魂的庇護所。」

280 #

You cannot have youth and the knowledge of it at the same time;

For youth is too busy living to know, and knowledge is too busy seeking itself to live. You may sit at your window watching the passersby. And watching you may see a nun walking toward your right hand, and a prostitute toward your left hand.

And you may say in your innocence, "How noble is the one and how ignoble is the other."

But should you close your eyes and listen awhile you would hear a voice whispering in the ether, "One seeks me in prayer, and the other in pain. And in the spirit of each there is a bower for my spirit."

283 #

一顆淌著血，另一顆堅忍不拔。

偉人有兩顆心；

282 #

願主餵養不虞匱乏之人！

281 #

每逢百年，拿撒勒的耶穌就會與基督教的耶穌在黎巴嫩山丘花園相會。

他們促膝長談；拿撒勒的耶穌道別前，每每都對基督教的耶穌說：

「朋友啊，我只怕我們永遠無法達成共識。」

281 #

Once every hundred years Jesus of Nazareth meets Jesus of the Christian in a garden among the hills of Lebanon. And they talk long; and each time Jesus of Nazareth goes away saying to Jesus of the Christian, "My friend, I fear we shall never, never agree."

282 #

May God feed the over-abundant!

283 #

A great man has two hearts; one bleeds and the other forbears.

## 284 #

Should one tell a lie which does not hurt you nor anyone else, why not say in your heart that the house of his facts is too small for his fancies, and he had to leave it for larger space?

## 285 #

Behind every closed door is a mystery sealed with seven seals.

## 286 #

Waiting is the hoofs of time.

## 286 #

等待是時間的蹄。

## 285 #

每扇緊閉門扉後方，都鎖著一個七重封印的祕密。

## 284 #

若有人撒了一個無傷大雅的謊，何不在你心裡說，他裝載事實的屋子小到裝不下想像，所以得把想像留給遼闊空間？

290 #
必將我們的露水與眼淚一飲而盡。
偉大上帝口乾舌燥之際，

289 #
我們的淚水跟大海裡都有它。
鹽巴肯定有其神聖奧妙之處。

288 #
卻永遠忘不了跟你一起哭的人。
你可能會淡忘跟你一起笑的人，

287 #
若麻煩成為你屋舍東牆的一塊新窗，該如何是好？

287 #

What if trouble should be a new window in the Eastern wall of your house?

288 #

You may forget the one with whom you have laughed, but never the one
with whom you have wept.

289 #

There must be something strangely sacred in salt. It is in our tears and in the sea.

290 #

Our God in His gracious thirst will drink us all, the dewdrop and the tear.

293 #
若我是你，就不會在低潮時挑大海的錯。
這艘船狀況良好，船長能幹；
唯一錯亂失序的只有你的胃。

292 #
若你能夠站在種族國家與自我一個腕尺外的高度，
就真宛如上帝。

291 #
你只是龐大自我的一小塊碎片，
一張尋覓麵包的嘴，
一隻舉起水杯餵養乾涸之嘴的盲從之手。

## 291 #

You are but a fragment of your giant self, a mouth that seeks bread, and a blind hand that holds the cup for a thirsty mouth.

## 292 #

If you would rise but a cubit above race and country and self you would indeed become godlike.

## 293 #

If I were you I would not find fault with the sea at low tide.
It is a good ship and our Captain is able; it is only your stomach that is in disorder.

294 #

若你能坐在雲朵上，就不會看見國與國之間的邊界，也不會發現田與田之間的界石。

可惜了你不能坐在雲朵上。

295 #

七個世紀以前，七隻白鴿從深谷翩然翱翔至雪白山峰。

七個男人望見牠們飛翔，其中一人說：

「我瞥見第七隻白鴿羽翼上有塊黑點。」

今日那座深谷裡的人，

都訴說著七隻黑鴿飛向白雪山峰的故事。

## 294 #

Should you sit upon a cloud you would not see the boundary line between one country and another, nor the boundary stone between a farm and a farm.

It is a pity you cannot sit upon a cloud.

## 295 #

Seven centuries ago seven white doves rose from a deep valley flying to the snow-white summit of the mountain. One of the seven men who watched the flight said, "I see a black spot on the wing of the seventh dove."

Today the people in that valley tell of seven black doves who flew to the summit of the snowy mountain.

## 297 #

若我向人伸出空蕩的手，卻沒有回饋，確實悲慘；
但伸出滿溢之手，卻無人可施，豈不更令人絕望。

## 296 #

秋季降臨，我將憂愁收好，在我的庭院裡深埋。

四月歸返，春天與大地結合，庭院裡長滿美麗出眾的花朵。

鄰居前來觀賞花兒，對我說：「下一次秋季播種的時節，能否給我們花的種子，好讓我們也能在庭院種出這些花？」

## 296 #

In the autumn I gathered all my sorrows and buried them in my garden.

And when April returned and spring came to wed the earth, there grew in my garden beautiful flowers unlike all other flowers.

And my neighbors came to behold them, and they all said to me, "When autumn comes again, at seeding time, will you not give us of the seeds of these flowers that we may have them in our gardens?"

## 297 #

It is indeed misery if I stretch an empty hand to men and receive nothing; but it is hopelessness if I stretch a full hand and find none to receive.

## 298 #

I long for eternity because there I shall meet my unwritten poems and my unpainted pictures.

## 299 #

Art is a step from nature toward the Infinite.

## 300 #

A work of art is a mist carved into an image.

## 301 #

Even the hands that make crowns of thorns are better than idle hands.

301 #

編織荊棘皇冠的雙手，都比無所事事的手好。

300 #

藝術作品就是刻印成影像的迷霧。

299 #

藝術就是從大自然通往無垠的一步台階。

298 #

我盼望永恆，因為我能在那裡遇見我尚未著墨的詩詞，我從未抒發的畫作。

305 #
猶大母親對他的愛，可會少於馬利亞對耶穌的愛？

304 #
若耶穌的曾孫知曉自己的血脈，難道不會對自己敬畏三分？

303 #
每個人都是曾經存在的國王與奴隸的後代子嗣。

302 #
最神聖的淚水從不湧上雙眼。

## 302 #

Our most sacred tears never seek our eyes.

## 303 #

Every man is the descendant of every king and every slave that ever lived.

## 304 #

If the great-grandfather of Jesus had known what was hidden within him, would he not have stood in awe of himself?

## 305 #

Was the love of Judas' mother of her son less than the love of Mary for Jesus?

## 307 #

## 306 #

關於我們的兄弟耶穌，有三件聖經未記載的奇蹟：

第一，他跟你我一樣皆為凡人，

第二，他有幽默感，

第三，他知道即使他輸了，事實上是贏的。

受難的你，在我內心的十字架上處死；

刺穿你手掌的釘子，也穿透我的心牆。

明日陌生人行經各各他時，不會知曉有兩人曾在此淌血。

他只會當那是一人的血。

## 306 #

There are three miracles of our Brother Jesus not yet recorded in the Book:
the first that He was a man like you and me, the second that He had a sense of
humour, and the third that He knew He was a conqueror though conquered.

## 307 #

Crucified One, you are crucified upon my heart; and the nails that pierce your
hands pierce the walls of my heart.
And tomorrow when a stranger passes by this Golgotha he will not know that
two bled here.

## 308 #

You may have heard of the Blessed Mountain.

It is the highest mountain in our world.

Should you reach the summit you would have only one desire, and that to

descend and be with those who dwell in the deepest valley.

That is why it is called the Blessed Mountain.


## 309 #

Every thought I have imprisoned in expression I must free by my deeds.


## 308 #

你可能聽過福山，那是世界最高峰。

若你抵達峰頂，就只會有一個欲望，

那就是下山，跟住在深丘壑谷的人們生活。

這就是它之所以為福山的原因。


## 309 #

每個我無法表達的禁錮思想，

都必藉由我的行動自由解放。

**國家圖書館出版品預行編目資料**

沙與沫 / 哈利勒 . 紀伯倫 (Khalil Gibran) 著；
張家綺譯 . -- 初版 . -- 臺中市：好讀，2017.09

面；　公分 . -- ( 典藏經典 )

ISBN 978-986-178-420-5( 平裝 )

865.751　　　106003096

### 好讀出版

典藏經典 106

## 沙與沫【中英對照版】

作　　者／紀伯倫（Khalil Gibran）
譯　　者／張家綺
總 編 輯／鄧茵茵
文字編輯／莊銘桓
內頁編排／鄭年亨
行銷企劃／劉恩綺
發 行 所／好讀出版有限公司
臺中市 407 西屯區何厝里 19 鄰大有街 13 號
TEL:04-23157795　FAX:04-23144188
http://howdo.morningstar.com.tw
（如對本書編輯或內容有意見，請來電或上網告訴我們）
法律顧問／陳思成律師

戶名：知己圖書股份有限公司
劃撥帳號：15060393
服務專線：04-23595819 轉 230
傳真專線：04-23597123
E-mail：service@morningstar.com.tw
如需詳細出版書目、訂書，歡迎洽詢
晨星網路書店 http://www.morningstar.com.tw

印刷／上好印刷股份有限公司 TEL:04-23150280
初版／西元 2017 年 9 月 15 日
定價：200 元
如有破損或裝訂錯誤，請寄回臺中市 407 工業區 30 路 1 號更換（好讀倉儲部收）

Published by How Do Publishing Co., LTD.
2017 Printed in Taiwan
ISBN 978-986-178-420-5
All rights reserved.

# 讀者回函

只要寄回本回函，就能不定時收到晨星出版集團最新電子報及相關優惠活動訊息，並有機會參加抽獎，獲得贈書。因此有電子信箱的讀者，千萬別忘於寫上你的信箱地址

書名：**沙與沫【中英對照版】**

姓名：＿＿＿＿＿＿＿＿　性別：□男□女　生日：＿＿＿年＿＿＿月＿＿＿日

教育程度：＿＿＿＿＿＿＿＿＿＿＿＿＿

職業：□學生 □教師 □一般職員 □企業主管
　　　□家庭主婦 □自由業 □醫護 □軍警 □其他＿＿＿＿＿＿＿＿＿＿＿

電子郵件信箱（e-mail）：＿＿＿＿＿＿＿＿＿＿＿ 電話：＿＿＿＿＿＿＿＿

聯絡地址：□□□＿＿＿＿＿＿＿＿＿＿＿＿＿＿＿＿＿＿＿＿＿＿＿

你怎麼發現這本書的？

□書店 □網路書店（哪一個？）＿＿＿＿＿＿＿＿＿ □朋友推薦 □學校選書

□報章雜誌報導 □其他＿＿＿＿＿＿＿＿＿＿＿＿＿＿＿＿＿＿＿＿＿＿

買這本書的原因是：＿＿＿＿＿＿＿＿＿＿＿＿＿＿＿＿＿＿＿＿＿＿＿＿

□內容題材深得我心 □價格便宜 □封面與內頁設計很優 □其他＿＿＿＿＿

你對這本書還有其他意見嗎？請通通告訴我們：

＿＿＿＿＿＿＿＿＿＿＿＿＿＿＿＿＿＿＿＿＿＿＿＿＿＿＿＿＿＿＿＿＿＿

你希望能如何得到更多好讀的出版訊息？

□常寄電子報 □網站常常更新 □常在報章雜誌上看到好讀新書消息

□我有更棒的想法＿＿＿＿＿＿＿＿＿＿＿＿＿＿＿＿＿＿＿＿＿＿＿＿＿＿

是否能與我們分享您嗜好閱讀的類型呢？

□文學/小說□社科/史哲□健康/醫療□科普□自然□寵物□旅遊□生活/娛樂

□心理/勵志□宗教/命理□設計/生活雜藝□財經/商管□語言/學習□親子/

童書□圖文/插畫□兩性/情慾□其他

我們確實接收到你對好讀的心意了，再次感謝你抽空填寫這份回函，請有空時上網或來信與我們交換意見，好讀出版有限公司編輯部同仁感謝你！

好讀的部落格：http://howdo.morningstar.com.tw/

好讀的粉絲團：https://www.facebook.com/howdobooks

填寫本回函，代表您接受好讀出版及相關企業，不定期提供給您相關出版及活動資訊，謝謝您！

請填妥後對折黏貼，直接投郵即可，無須貼郵票。

# 好讀出版有限公司 編輯部收

407 台中市西屯區何厝里大有街 13 號
電話：04-23157795-6　傳真：04-23144188

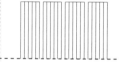

-------------------- 沿虛線對折 --------------------

## 購買好讀出版書籍的方法：

一、先請你上晨星網路書店 http://www.morningstar.com.tw 檢索
　　書目
　　或直接在網上購買

二、以郵政劃撥購書：帳號 15060393 戶名：知己圖書股份有限公司
　　並在通信欄中註明你想買的書名與數量

三、大量訂購者可直接以客服專線洽詢，有專人為您服務：
　　客服專線：04-23595819 轉 230　傳真：04-23597123

四、客服信箱：service@morningstar.com.tw